Three Little Pigs

A Traditional English Folktale   **Illustrated by Saburo Yamada**

R.I.C. Publications
Dublin • London • Perth • Tokyo

Once upon a time, there lived a mother pig and her three little pigs.

The mother pig was so poor, she could no longer keep them all. She had to send them out to make their own way in the world. As she said goodbye to each little pig, she said, "Be careful of the big bad wolf!"

The first little pig to leave home met a man carrying a big bale of straw.

The little pig asked him, "Please, could I have that straw so that I can build my house?"

The man gave him the straw, and the little pig built a straw house with it.

Just as he was settling in, along came a wolf who knocked at the door and said, "Little pig, little pig, let me come in."

The pig answered, "Not by the hair on my chinny-chin-chin."

"Then I'll huff, and I'll puff, and I'll blow your house down."

So the wolf huffed and he puffed, and he blew down the flimsy house and ate up the little pig.

The second little pig met a man carrying a bundle of sticks.

"Please, could you give me those sticks so that I can build my house?"

The man gave him the sticks, and the little pig built his house.

Then along came the wolf and said, "Little pig, little pig, let me come in."

"Not by the hair on my chinny-chin-chin."

"Then I'll huff and I'll puff, and I'll blow your house down."

So, he huffed and he puffed, and he huffed and he puffed, and he blew the wobbly house down and ate up the little pig.

The third little pig met a man moving a load of bricks. The pig asked him, "Please, could you give me some bricks so that I can build my house?"

The pig was given a large pile of bricks and used them to build his house.

Before long, the wolf came up to the front door and said, "Little pig, little pig, let me come in."

"Not by the hair on my chinny-chin-chin."

"Then I'll huff and I'll puff and I'll blow your house down."

Well, he huffed and he puffed, and he puffed and he huffed, and he huffed and he puffed ... but no matter how hard he tried, he could not blow the sturdy brick house down.

So, he said, "Listen little pig. I know where there's a great field of turnips. It's out behind Farmer John's place. If you'd like, I'll come by tomorrow and we can go pick some together."

"Great, I'll come. What time will you be going?"

"Oh, say around six."

So, the little pig got up at five and picked a bunch of turnips and got home safely before the wolf came by at six.

"Little pig, are you ready to go?"

"I've already been there, and picked a big basket full of juicy turnips!"

When he heard this, the wolf was very angry. But he was determined to somehow catch the little pig, so he said, "Say, little pig, I know where there's a tree with delicious red apples."

"Where's that?"

"At the bottom of the park. If you promise not to fool me this time, I'll come pick you up at five and we can go and pick some apples."

So, the little pig got up at four in the morning, and hurried off to pick some apples. The park was a fair distance and the little pig had to climb the tree to pick the apples, so before he could finish, the wolf had arrived. The little pig was frightened out of his wits!

The wolf came near and said, "Well, well, little pig. You've arrived before me. How are the apples?"

"They're quite good. Here, I'll throw one down for you."

The little pig threw an apple as far as he could. As the wolf ran off over the hill to pick it up, the little pig jumped down from the tree and quickly ran back home.

The next day, the wolf came back again and said, "Little pig, this afternoon there's going to be a fair in town. Would you like to come?"

"Sure, I'll go. What time do you plan to leave?"

"At three," the wolf answered.

So, the little pig left well before then and saw the fair, bought a butter churn, and started back home with the churn on his back. But then he spotted the wolf coming towards him. The little pig didn't know what to do. When he jumped into the butter churn to hide, it fell over and started to roll down the hill, right towards the wolf, with the little pig still inside. The wolf was so terrified that he didn't even stop to see the fair, but ran all the way home.

Later that day, the wolf went over to the little pig's house and told him that something big and round had come rolling down upon him and just about frightened him to death.

Then the little pig said, "Ha, ha! That would have been me who frightened you! I went to the fair, bought a butter churn, and when you came along, I jumped into the churn and rolled down the hill."

When he heard this, the wolf was enraged and shouted, "You scoundrel, I'll get you yet! I'm coming down your chimney to eat you up!"

The little pig quickly filled a large pot with water, and built a roaring fire beneath it. Just as the wolf was coming down the chimney, the little pig lifted the lid off the cauldron and the wolf fell into the water with a big splash.

In an instant, the little pig put the lid on the pot again. He boiled the wolf and ate him for dinner. The little pig lived happily ever after.

Illustrator

Saburo Yamada was born in Tokyo in 1927. Through his work in a puppet studio and participation in the rebuilding of the puppet theatre group, Puk, he devoted himself to puppet theatre and puppet movies. Later, he produced illustrations for numerous works. His picture books include *A Fox and Field Mice*, and *The Sly Fox and the Clever Duck*, published by Fukuinkan Shoten Publishers. He died in 1979.

Three Little Pigs

Illustrations © Saburo Yamada 1960

First published by Fukuinkan Shoten Publishers, Inc., Tokyo, Japan.

Re-published under licence
by R.I.C. Publications Limited Asia,
Tokyo, Japan

Japanese ISBN: 978 4 902216 15 8
International ISBN: 978 1 74126 031 1

Printed in Japan

Distributed by:

Asia

R.I.C. Publications – Asia
5th Floor, Gotanda Mikado Building,
2–5–8 Hiratsuka, Shinagawa-Ku Tokyo,
Japan 142–0051
Tel: (03) 3788 9201
Email: elt@ricpublications.com
Website: www.ricpublications.com

Australasia

R.I.C. Publications
PO Box 332
Greenwood
Western Australia 6924
Tel: (618) 9240 9888

United Kingdom and Ireland

Prim-Ed Publishing
Bosheen
New Ross
Co. Wexford, Ireland
Tel: (353) 514 40075

R.I.C.Story Chest
三びきのこぶた（英語版）
Three Little Pigs
2004年11月30日発行
2007年8月20日第2版

イギリス民話
絵 山田三郎

発行者 ジョン・ムーア
発行所 アールアイシー出版株式会社
〒142-0051
東京都品川区平塚2-5-8
五反田ミカドビル5F
Tel:(03)3788-9201
Fax:(03)3788-9202

ISBN 978-4-902216-15-8
http://www.ricpublications.com
Printed in Japan